JE YAM

Yamaka, Sara.

The gift of Driscoll
Lipscomb /

WITHDRAWN

CENTRAL - J

D0938570

The GIFT of DRISCOLL LIPSCOMB

by **Sara Yamaka**

illustrated by **Joung Un Kim**

Simon & Schuster Books for Young Readers

SIMON & SCHUSTER BOOKS FOR YOUNG READERS An imprint of Simon & Schuster Children's Publishing Division, 1230 Avenue of the Americas, New York, NY 10020. Text copyright © 1995 by Sara Yamaka. Illustrations copyright © 1995 by Joung Un Kim. All rights reserved including the right of reproduction in whole or in part in any form. SIMON & SCHUSTER BOOKS FOR YOUNG READERS is a trademark of Simon & Schuster. Designed by Christy Hale. The text of this book is set in Tiffany. The illustrations are rendered in acrylic. Manufactured in the United States of America 10 9 8 7 6 5 4 3 2 1 Library of Congress Cataloging-in-Publication Data Yamaka, Sara. The gift of Driscoll Lipscomb / by Sara Yamaka ; illustrated by Joung Un Kim.—1st ed. p. cm. Summary: Molly learns about the beauty of the world around her from Driscoll Lipscomb, a painter who gives her a pot of paint in a different color of the rainbow each year on her birthday. [1. Rainbows—Fiction.] I. Kim, Joung Un, ill. II. Title. Pz7.Y1914Gi 1995 [E]—dc20 93-43207 ISBN 0-02-793599-X

To my parents and
for Stephanie Yamaka
and Kevin Yamaka
—S.Y.

For Mom and Dad,
Joung Youp, Tae Un,
and Eddie
—J.U.K.

Driscoll Lipscomb was a friend of mine many years ago. He used to invite me to his house to see the wonderful paintings that he made. The house of Driscoll Lipscomb smelled of turpentine and oil paint, and inside it always looked like the sun was out after a rain.

"In every painting I put a rainbow, Molly," Driscoll would say. "A rainbow for you."

And in each corner Driscoll Lipscomb would sign his name with a long, swirling $\mathcal{L}$.

When I turned four, Driscoll gave me a brush and a pot of red paint. And for one year I painted tomatoes and apples and roses alongside Driscoll Lipscomb. I wondered, Why did he give me red?

When I turned five, Driscoll gave me a brush and a pot of orange paint. And for one year I painted tangerines and beach balls and orange-flavored lollipops alongside Driscoll Lipscomb. I looked at the orange and red together and I saw the colors smile.

When I turned six, Driscoll gave me a brush and a pot of yellow paint. And for one year I painted suns and sunsets and lemons alongside Driscoll Lipscomb. I felt the warmth of my summer sun, even though my birthday is in November.

When I turned seven, Driscoll gave me a brush and a pot of green paint. And for one year I painted leaves and limes and shiny green beetles alongside Driscoll Lipscomb. My grass seemed to ripple across the canvas.

When I turned eight, Driscoll gave me a brush and a pot of blue paint. And for one year I painted the sky and the sea and blueberry pie alongside Driscoll Lipscomb.

And I gathered my pots together and saw Driscoll's gift.

And when I turned nine, Driscoll gave me a brush and a pot of violet paint, and he said, "Now, Molly, you have the rainbow. Do with it what you want. Paint your dreams."

So I went to hillsides and stream banks at dawn and dusk and noon to paint. At dawn the red was russet and the yellow burning hot, and the violet lay delicate and wistful. At dusk a misty gray seeped into blue, and the orange deepened into pumpkin color. At noon the brilliance of the blue and the cleanness of the green were lighted by a clear, strong, orange-yellow.

And I took my paints, my gift, and I worked.

I worked for a long time . . . for many
misty dusks and clear dawns and brilliant
noons. I saw the violet on the wing tip
of a bird and the green beetle at my feet.

Soon Driscoll Lipscomb was a very old man, and most people trod softly around him. But I knew Driscoll, and so I went to see him one November, on my twelfth birthday. We talked of paintings and good times, and I had to leave too soon.

"Good-bye, Driscoll."

"Good-bye, Molly. Do you now see?"

"What?" I asked.

Driscoll only smiled.

But then I stepped out into a lemon-and-blueberry day. I saw a violet blue balloon bobbing down the sandy street, attached to a peachy boy in a forest green coat. Everything around me was colored with Driscoll's rainbow.

Then I laughed aloud and turned to run inside to say what I then knew. But there on the step stood Driscoll Lipscomb.

"So you see?" he asked.

"I *see*," I said.

And so I did—and do—see
the gift of Driscoll Lipscomb.